MW01042371

Cosmo
THE DODO BIRD™

Cosmo
THE DODO BIRD™

Cosmo is a dodo bird, a unique species that lived on Earth
300 years ago. Cosmo lived with his family and beloved
friends on the island of Mauritius, a paradise isolated from
the world known to man.

When the first humans arrived on the island, the dodos'
environment changed vastly, and it wasn't long before
almost all of the dodos completely disappeared.

Now, Cosmo is the last of his kind on Earth.

3RV

3R-V is a small robot-spaceship from the future, built to save extinct species. During his very first mission, he accidentally landed on Mauritius and met Cosmo, the last of the dodos. They decided that they would travel the universe looking for dodos. They found many adventures along the way, but did they find any dodos? Read and find out!

Les Aventures de Cosmo le dodo: La Tempête I names, characters, and related indicia are trademarks of Racine et Associés Inc. All Rights Reserved.

Originally published as *Les Aventures de Cosmo le dodo: La Tempête I* by Origo Publications, POB 4 Chambly, Quebec J3L 4B1, 2008

Copyright © 2009 by Racine et Associés
Concept created by Pat Rac.
Editing and Illustrations: Pat Rac
Writing Team: Joannie Beaudet, Neijib Bentaieb, François Perras, Pat Rac

English translation copyright © 2011 by Tundra Books
This English edition published in Canada by Tundra Books, 2011
75 Sherbourne Street, Toronto, Ontario M5A 2P9

Published in the United States by Tundra Books of Northern New York,
P.O. Box 1030, Plattsburgh, New York 12901

Library of Congress Control Number: 2010928802

All rights reserved. The use of any part of this publication reproduced, transmitted in any form or by any means, electronic, mechanical, photocopying, recording, or otherwise, or stored in a retrieval system, without the prior written consent of the publisher – or, in case of photocopying or other reprographic copying, a licence from the Canadian Copyright Licensing Agency – is an infringement of the copyright law.

Library and Archives Canada Cataloguing in Publication
Pat Rac, 1963-
[Tempête I. English]
The climate masters / Patrice Racine.

(The Aventures of Cosmo the dodo bird)
Translation of: La tempête I.

ISBN 978-1-77049-243-1
I. Title. II. Title: Tempête I. English. III. Series: Pat Rac, 1963- .
Aventures of Cosmo the Dodo Bird.

PS8631.A8294T4413 2011   jC843'.6   C2010-903176-8

We acknowledge the financial support of the Government of Canada through the Book Publishing Industry Development Program (BPIDP) and that of the Government of Ontario through the Ontario Media Development Corporation's Ontario Book Initiative. We further acknowledge the support of the Canada Council for the Arts and the Ontario Arts Council for our publishing program.

ONTARIO ARTS COUNCIL
CONSEIL DES ARTS DE L'ONTARIO

For more information on the international rights, please visit www.cosmothedodobird.com

Printed in Mexico

1 2 3 4 5 6   16 15 14 13 12 11

MIX
Paper from
responsible sources
FSC® C101537

For all the children of the world

THE ADVENTURES OF
Cosmo
THE DODO BIRD™

THE CLIMATE MASTERS

TUNDRA BOOKS

Table of Contents

CHAPTER ONE

A Perfect Day

It was a perfect day for looking into space. I peered through the lens of the telescope while 3R-V took notes in the planet's log. To tell the truth, there wasn't much to note, except for some distant stars. That is, until I saw something curious. "3R-V, look!"

"What do you see, Cosmo?"

"Not one, but two planets, 3R-V! Two planets!"

The two-heads was busy watering its hope flowers, but when it heard my excited cry, it hurried over to the telescope to have a look. The left head peered through the lens, then grabbed the log from 3R-V and scribbled some quick calculations.

"There are definitely two planets out there," Left said.

"*Yippee!* New planets to explore. Let's go, 3R-V!" I yelled.

"Cosmo, calm down. There's no need to hurry!" the left head said with a laugh. "I estimate that we'll be orbiting the planets for a few days."

As I climbed aboard 3R-V, I felt something tickling the soles of my feet. I turned to see Fabrico holding a broom.

"Fabrico, what are you doing?"

"It's cleanup week!" he said. "Did you forget?"

"Can't it wait? Why don't you come with us to explore the planets?"

"There's too much to do! And since no one is helping me . . ." Fabrico looked pointedly at Diggs.

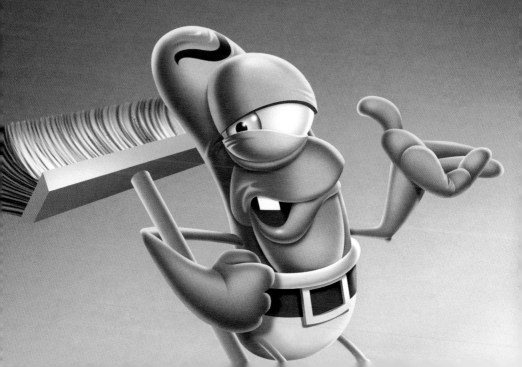

Fabrico went back to sweeping.

"What are you up to, Diggs?" I asked.

"My helmet is broken," Diggs told me as he rummaged through a pile of scrap metal.

"Are you coming with us? There are two new planets for us to explore," I pressed.

"No," Diggs answered. "*Grrr!* Now where is that miserable part?"

"Please come," said 3R-V. "It'll be an adventure."

"Can't, and that's that. Without my helmet, how am I going to travel in space?"

Diggs picked up a piece of metal and turned it every which way. He tried to cram it into his helmet, but it didn't fit.

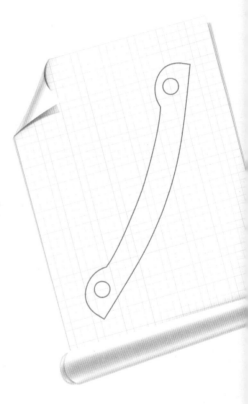

"What blasted luck!" he snorted. "I'm giving up, at least for now. If you find a metal rod that looks like this, could you bring it to me? I'm going to the beach! And don't say anything to Fabrico. *Grrr!* Him and his cleaning!" He snorted again and stomped off.

CHAPTER TWO

From the Storm

3R-V and I headed off.

"I sure hope that we find dodos on one of these planets!"

"I'm crossing my fingers for you," said 3R-V.

Suddenly, I saw a frightening sight.

"3R-V, watch out! A fireball is charging straight for us."

The robot-ship veered. We spun around in space
for a few seconds. The fireball disappeared behind us.

"That was too close for comfort," said 3R-V,
relieved.

"What do you think it was?"

"Probably a small meteor." 3R-V didn't sound sure.

The first planet loomed in front of us. It was surrounded by thick, black storm clouds. 3R-V entered its atmosphere down.

"I don't like the look of that storm," he said. Despite his misgivings, 3R-V dashed through the clouds. We were tossed and turned by the turbulence. Dizzy, I closed my eyes and gripped my seat.

We got through the clouds and were met with wind, lightning, and rain. Everything on the planet was in utter chaos. In order to cause such ruin, the storm must have raged for days.

"3R-V, what do you suppose happened here?"

"I have no idea!" replied 3R-V. "One thing is certain. I can't land."

"I agree. Anyway, no dodo would be able to survive here with such a terrible storm. Steer us to the second planet!"

CHAPTER THREE

Falling From the Sky

Back on our traveling planet, the two-heads was busy as usual: the scientific left head was making notes and the artistic right head was writing a poem.

A thought occurred to the right head. "Fabrico's cleaning the laboratory! He's so clumsy – what if he spills your potions?"

"Gee, I never thought of that!" Left looked over at Fabrico. The purple fellow was dusting the laboratory with a feather duster.

"There doesn't seem to be any danger," Left replied. "Anyway, none of the substances in my laboratory are poisonous or explosive."

"No danger, huh?" said a rattled right head.

How did Fabrico cause that explosion? Left wondered.

The two-heads looked at the damage. The laboratory had disappeared, and in its place was an enormous hole. Beyond the hole, Fabrico lay still on the ground.

"Fabrico, Fabrico!" both heads called. "Are you okay?"

Fabrico staggered to his feet. His face was covered with soot. His feather duster was singed.

"Ye . . . ye . . . ye . . . yes," he stammered.

"What have you done?" demanded the left head.

"You are clumsier than a giant monster in a field of china flowers!" said the poetic right head.

"I didn't do anything!" said Fabrico.

"Then how did this happen?" the heads asked.

"A fireball fell from space!"

"A fireball? Are you sure?" asked Left.

"Yes, I'm sure!"

The two-heads picked up a piece of broken beaker.

"My experiment is damaged beyond repair!" said Left.

"Oh, no!" exclaimed Right. "Do you mean the experiment with the little red flower that we picked from the top of the mountain?"

"Yes, that's the one. I know you have trouble sleeping, so I was making a potion to help you. I don't like the idea of having to climb that mountain again. It's the highest one on our planet."

"Don't worry. Fabrico will climb the mountain instead."

"But . . ." said the purple fellow.

"This mess is your fault, Fabrico!" said the heads.

Fabrico started to object, but he looked at the heads' firm faces, and decided against it. As he set off to the mountain, Right and Left could hear him grumbling, "Life is unfair."

"What a mess. We'll be cleaning up for days," said Left as the two-heads looked at the damage.

"Look!" shouted Right. "There's something in the hole!"

A mysterious fire flickered at the bottom of the crater.

"That must be the fireball!" exclaimed the left head.

"Fabrico was telling the truth. The explosion wasn't his fault – a fireball made this mess," said the right head. "I think it's still dangerous. This isn't the time for Fabrico to climb a mountain. Let's go warn him."

The two-heads was about to follow Fabrico, but it couldn't take its eyes off the flickering fireball. When the flames died down, an object was left on the ground. The two-heads looked at each other, and, a moment later, the creature leapt down into the crater.

"What is it?" asked the right head, reaching out a hand.

"Don't touch it!" cried the left head. "It could still be hot enough to burn!"

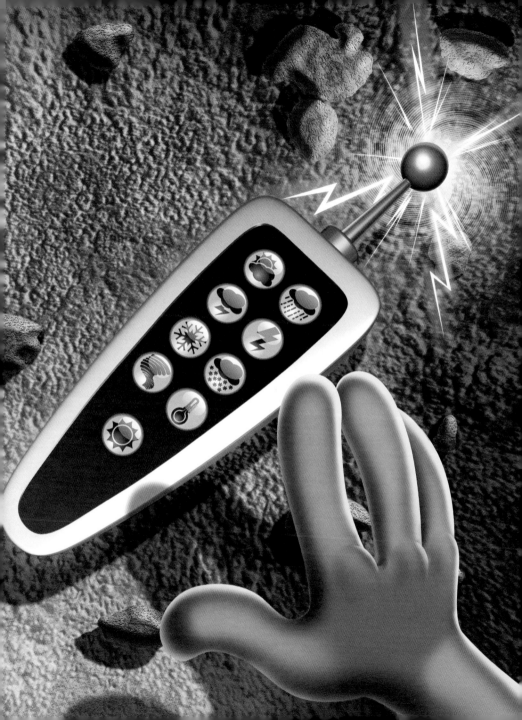

But it was too late. Right had already picked up the object. "Amazing! It's cold!" the right head cried.

The two-heads examined the object from every angle.

"It looks like a remote control," said Left.

The two-heads climbed out of the crater with the remote control.

"Look at all the beautiful symbols, Left. They look like pieces of art."

"They look like buttons." Left wasn't interested in art. He wanted to know where the object came from and what it was for. "Let's see what it does."

Right pressed one of the buttons.

CHAPTER FOUR

Messy Weather

Suddenly, the heavens were covered in a gray cloud. The bright day darkened. A snowflake landed on the left head's nose. It was snowing!

"Incredible!" the heads said together.

The left head studied the different symbols on the remote, while snowflakes fell all around. "That symbol looks like a sun," Left said, pressing the button. The clouds vanished.

"This remote–" began Right.

"Controls the climate!" finished Left.

The left head pointed the device upwards and pressed a button with a rain cloud painted on it. Right away, drops of water began to fall.

"How is this possible?" asked the left head.

The two-heads danced in the rain.

Left scrunched up his eyes and thought hard. Right grabbed the object and pressed the rain button again.

"It's raining harder," cried Left. "What did you do?"

"I pressed the rain button again."

The two-heads couldn't see through the heavy curtain of rain.

"This remote even controls how hard the rain falls," said Left, as the two-heads took a soggy step. "Will you look at all this mud! Fabrico's not going to like this. You know how he feels about cleanliness."

"Oh no, Fabrico!" cried both heads. They had forgotten about their purple friend.

"He's out searching for the red flower in all this rain," said Right.

"Get rid of all the clouds," ordered Left. "We have to find him."

Right pressed the sun button, and the weather cleared up. But bringing out the sun was so much fun that both heads soon forgot about Fabrico again. They just couldn't stop playing with the device.

They pressed button after button and laughed at their power. Over and over, they made it rain, shine, and snow.

When Right grew tired of the game, Left took control of the remote. The sun was shining, but he pressed the snowflake button while pointing the remote at the telescope. Snow began to fall on it.

"Just as I thought," Left said. "You can change the climate in another area without it affecting you."

"Let me try!" While Right amused himself, making it snow over a rock and rain over a field of hope flowers, Left took notes on a blackboard.

"This is great," Right said proudly. "I can water the hope flowers without doing a bit of work!"

Left was too busy with numbers to pay attention, and that annoyed the right head. He pointed the remote control at Left and pressed the rain button.

"Right, what have you done?" cried Left angrily. "You have messed up my calculations!" The more Left yelled, the more Right laughed.

Left snatched the remote and pointed it at Right. He jabbed a button and a snow cloud formed above Right's head. Left burst out laughing.

Right snatched the remote back and aimed it at Left again. This time, pushing the snow button twice to create a storm.

"Hey!" yelled the left head.

Left grabbed for the device, but Right held it out of reach and said "I'm the one who gets to control the climate!"

"Give me that remote!" cried Left.

"No!" snapped Right.

"You are so stubborn!" shouted Left. He twisted Right's nose until Right dropped the remote. Left grabbed it and punched the snow button over and over until the right head was encased in ice. "Who's in control now?" he shouted.

Suddenly, a lightning bolt struck the remote, and it fell to the ground. The two-heads reached for it, but nothing happened. Left was stunned by lightning and Right was frozen stiff.

A day passed. Then two days. Cold rain continued to fall on Left, while it snowed on Right. The two stubborn heads were in a deadlock.

CHAPTER FIVE

Without Life

3R-V and I knew none of this was happening. We were far from our traveling home. We'd left the first stormy planet and had spent a lot of time exploring the second planet.

"Cosmo, we have explored every corner of this place."

I looked around. The whole surface was littered with fallen trees. The ground was cracked, the riverbeds were dry, the sky was gray, and the wind was icy-cold.

I touched a tree trunk. The bark turned to dust and crumbled under my wing. I sneezed.

For the umpteenth time, 3R-V said "This planet is dead!"

My feathers stood on end.

I discovered a half-buried park bench. "Look, 3R-V. If somebody or something put a park bench here, this planet wasn't always this way. It must have been inhabited once."

"I guess," said 3R-V thoughtfully. "But today, nothing could live here. There's no water or sun or vegetation. It sure doesn't have the wandering planet's nice climate."

"And it's nothing like a tropical island." I thought of Earth, my long-lost warm, green home and swallowed back tears. "No dodo could survive here."

3R-V could see my disappointment. He asked, "How are you doing?"

"This is just a setback." I ruffled my feathers. "I won't give up my search for dodos. We'll find other planets and one of them will have dodos on it!"

We looked at the ruined landscape one last time,
and then we started back to the traveling planet that
was now our home.

CHAPTER SIX

Fabrico's Turn

Back home, the left head shivered in the rain, and the right head was frozen stiff from the snow. Their foreheads burned with fever, their noses were stuffed up, and their eyes were red, but they still wouldn't cooperate and end their misery.

"It's . . . my . . . remote control!" mumbled Right.

"It's mine!" sniffled Left.

They stopped when Fabrico appeared. "I have your red flower!" he shouted.

"Fabrico?" said the two-heads.

"What's going on here?" asked Fabrico. He picked up the remote control. "What's this?" It was only then that he noticed the heads and the mess they were in. "What trouble have you gotten into?"

"The remote control is responsible for everything!" explained Right.

"*Achoo!* It controls the climate," added Left.

"It has buttons to make it rain, snow, hail, and shine," continued the right head.

Fabrico studied the object in his hand.

"You were right, there was a fireball, and this was in its center," said Left.

Fabrico flung the red flower away. "I risked my life on that mountain for a punishment I didn't deserve! I told you that a fireball ruined your experiment, *not* me!" With that, Fabrico turned his back to the two-heads.

"Please forgive us, Fabrico," Right and Left mumbled sheepishly. "We're very sorry."

Left tried to explain. "We were going after you, but we got so caught up with playing with the remote that . . . um . . . we forgot about you." That only made things worse. Fabrico lifted his chin a little higher.

Now Right and Left were getting angry. They had apologized, and they wanted desperately to be warm and dry. "Stop being silly. We said we were sorry!" said Left. "Point the remote control toward our heads and press the sun button. Please!"

"Why should I help you? You didn't believe me and you forced me to climb an enormous mountain!"

The two-heads got to its knees before Fabrico.

"I'll do anything you say. I can't stand any more of this snow!" Right shivered.

"And I'm so wet from this rain that I'm growing moss," said Left.

Fabrico thought for a moment while the heads sniffed. "Will you help me with a big cleaning?"

The two-heads nodded.

Finally Fabrico gave in. "Well, the next time I say that I saw a fireball, you'd better believe me!" With that, he pointed the remote control at the two-heads and pressed a button. Instead of clearing up, the clouds merged, turning the rain and snow into hail.

"Oh no!" the heads cried.

"Oops!"

"Press the sun button, Fabrico! Quickly!" ordered Left.

Confused, the purple fellow pushed all of the buttons. Finally, the clouds disappeared and the sun shone.

The two-heads stretched and groaned. It was chilled through and through. It was hard for the creature to walk, but it made its way to the broom, nonetheless. With every step it took, the heads sneezed.

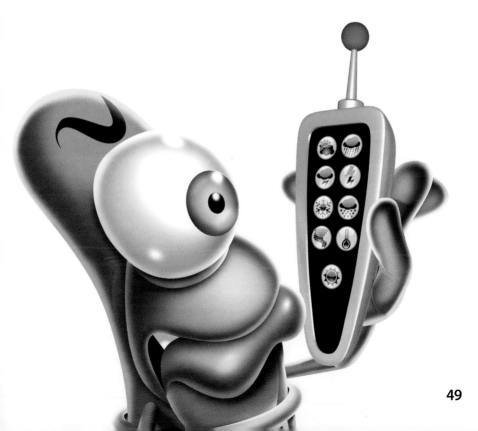

Fabrico dropped the remote control and began his favorite pastime – cleaning!

"*Oof!* All this old stuff is useless," Fabrico said to himself. He came across a mysterious red stick. "Well isn't this pretty? I wonder what it is." Fabrico twisted and turned his discovery. Then he touched a small button. To his great surprise, the object unfolded. "Wow! This is amazing. I love it!"

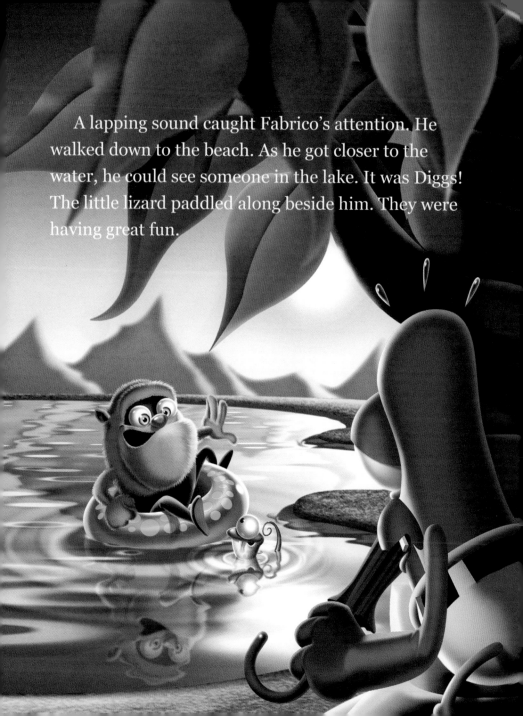

A lapping sound caught Fabrico's attention. He walked down to the beach. As he got closer to the water, he could see someone in the lake. It was Diggs! The little lizard paddled along beside him. They were having great fun.

So! Diggs was too busy to help me clean! thought Fabrico crossly. He was about to scold Diggs, when Fabrico remembered the remote control. He retraced his steps to fetch it.

He had an idea — one that made him laugh out loud.

CHAPTER SEVEN

Grrr!

Diggs shivered on his float. The sun that had warmed him had disappeared behind a small cloud right above him. "Lizard!" he shouted. Diggs pointed to where the sun was still shining. "Push me over there."

The little Lizard obeyed. But no sooner had she pushed Diggs into the sun, that the cloud was back above him. "Farther, Lizard, farther!"

The lizard swam back to Diggs and pushed him again, but the cloud followed Diggs.

"I don't get it!" he grumbled.

Suddenly, the cloud burst and rain poured down on Diggs. *"Grrr!"*

On the shore, Fabrico watched. He was enjoying himself. *"Ha, ha, ha!* What should I do next? *Ha, ha, ha!"*

Then, the water turned cold. The little lizard jumped on Diggs's head just as the lake began to freeze.

Though he thought nobody could hear him, Diggs cried out: "In the name of a twisted helmet, someone get me out of here!"

Diggs was so scared – scared stiff – that he couldn't budge. "Help! Help me!" he cried.

Fabrico rolled around on the ground, clutching his sides. "*Ha ha, ha!* This is hilarious. I have to try something else!"

The sun returned above Diggs. The ice melted, and Diggs was free at last. He swam to shore as fast as he could, and collapsed on the sand.

The sun was warming him up nicely. *Aaaah,* thought Diggs. But, gradually, he began to feel hotter . . . and hotter. Before long, the heat was unbearable. Diggs's skin turned bright red.

"Ouch!" he moaned.

A cloud appeared again. Diggs stood under it to get away from the blazing sunlight. No sooner did he feel comfortable, than the cloud darkened and it started to rain. Diggs ran back and forth on the beach, lightning crackling on his heels. No matter how fast he ran, he couldn't get out from under the cloud.

Fabrico laughed hysterically. He was so loud that Diggs heard him.

With the cloud still chasing him, he charged toward the sound of Fabrico's voice.

CHAPTER EIGHT

Master of the Situation

"Fabrico!?" he yelled.

"*Ha ha, ha!*" was the only reply. Fabrico pressed a button, and the storm cloud disappeared.

"Are you responsible for what's happening?" Diggs bellowed.

"*Ha ha, ha!* It's this remote control," Fabrico spluttered. "It controls the climate." Then he laughed again.

"What?!" Diggs stared at the device in Fabrico's hand. "How does that thing work?"

Fabrico showed off his treasure. "It's easy. You aim it. Then you press a button. Each one makes something different happen."

Diggs listened carefully, rubbing his chin.

"Oh, dear. Are you red from embarrassment or anger?" asked Fabrico. "Oops! I forgot. It's your sunburn! *Ha, ha, ha!*"

Diggs leapt at Fabrico and grabbed the device out of his hand.

"Hey!" Fabrico cried. "Give that back! It's mine!"

"No way!"

Fabrico rushed at Diggs. "It's *my* remote control! Give it back!"

Diggs aimed the remote at Fabrico and sent down a terrible lightning bolt. It crashed to the ground just as Fabrico jumped away. Diggs looked at the powerful object, amazed. He pointed it to the sky and tested all the possibilities: rain, storm, snow, and sunshine.

His eyes twinkled at the idea of such power. Fabrico touched his arm, but Diggs shrugged him off.

"Give me my remote control!" Fabrico whined in a small voice.

"Two tiny things to remember, Fabrico: One. It's now *my* remote control. Two. You may call me Master Diggs!"

Diggs climbed on a rock and aimed the remote. He pressed the rain button, cackling happily.

Fabrico remembered the pretty red contraption
he'd found. Unfurling it, he thought, *What a great
invention this is! It keeps me dry while it's raining.*

Soon, the two-heads appeared, complaining. All
the rain, snow, and hail weren't helping it get better.

"Fabrico, stop playing with the remote control!"
said Right.

"It's not me! I don't have the remote control anymore," Fabrico retorted.

"What do you mean! Did you lose it?" asked Left.

"No, I didn't lose it!" Fabrico was offended.

"Well then, where is it?" Left demanded.

Fabrico pointed upwards. Left and Right saw Diggs standing at the top of the cliff.

"SILENCE!" commanded Diggs.

The two-heads and Fabrico stared back at him, speechless.

"Bow down before Master Diggs. Otherwise, prepare for my wrath!"

CHAPTER NINE

Ha, Ha, Ha!

Aboard 3R-V, I watched until the dead planet disappeared into the distance. "Do you think a storm could have caused such damage?" I asked.

"Yes. Maybe the same storm that raged on the first planet visited here first," said 3R-V.

I nodded. "It's as if the storm was a sickness that infected these planets."

We thought about that possibility.

As we neared our traveling planet, we saw a disturbing sight. "Look at all the clouds that have gathered!" I said to 3R-V.

"How strange. The sun was shining when we left," said 3R-V.

"Oh no! What if our planet has caught the storm virus, too? I hope our friends are okay. Hurry, 3R-V! They may need our help!"

3R-V sped up until he was going as fast as he could. A blizzard raged on one side of the planet, but on the other side, the planet was hidden under sodden, gray rain clouds.

3R-V didn't know where to land. Then he saw a sunny opening between two rain clouds and rushed toward the gap. "Phew!" 3R-V said as he touched down.

Around us, rain fell, thunder roared, and lightning flashed.

"The storm has already begun!" I said to 3R-V as we rushed to find our friends.

We found Diggs at the top of a hill, the sun shining down on him. He looked scary. Even the little lizard had a nasty look.

"Is Diggs scheming again?" said 3R-V angrily. "What does he have in his hand? Look over there, Cosmo!" The two-heads and Fabrico were at the bottom of the hill. "Why are they bowing before Diggs?"

I was as puzzled as the robot-ship. "Let's find out!"

65

3R-V hovered close enough for us to hear Diggs's voice: "I am the Grand Master Diggs! Watch out for my lightning bolts!" That's when he saw us.

"Cosmo! 3R-V! What are you doing here?" Diggs growled.

3R-V landed, and I jumped out. Fabrico and the two-heads motioned for us to keep away from him. But I was not about to let Diggs scare me.

"I could ask you the same question! What are *you* doing up there? And why are the others afraid of you, Diggs?"

"You are to call me *Master* Diggs!"

"Why, on the traveling planet, would I do that?" I replied.

"Because I, Grand Master Diggs, possess the remote control!"

"What does the remote control do?"

"It controls the climate!" roared Diggs. With that, he pointed the device at 3R-V and me.

Diggs pressed one of the buttons on the remote.
An enormous lightning bolt came out of nowhere
and almost hit us.

"Bow down before the Grand Master of The
Traveling planet!"

SCRATCH!

"I'm not afraid of your lightning bolts!" said 3R-V bravely.

The robot-ship took a few steps toward Diggs. The little lizard stood in front of her owner and bared her fangs. *"Roooarr!"*

But 3R-V didn't back off.

"Stop, 3R-V!" shouted Diggs. But 3R-V kept going.

"You may be strong, 3R-V," Diggs cried, "but your friend is not!"

With that, he pointed his weapon at me. 3R-V leapt to my side to protect me.

"Aha! Now, 3R-V, join the others!" Diggs said gleefully.

"Diggs, listen to me," I said as calmly as I could.

He corrected me. "Grand Master Diggs!"

Gray clouds formed around us. Resigned, 3R-V and I climbed down the hill as Diggs laughed.

"*Ha ha ha*! You will all follow orders!" he shouted from the hilltop. He clutched the remote control in one hand.

CHAPTER TEN

Who's the Leader?

When we got to the foot of the hill, Fabrico and the
two-heads rushed to meet us.

"It's terrible, Cosmo!" the right head was scared.

So was the left head, who announced, "Diggs is
crazy! He won't stop the storms."

"Snowstorms!" Right shivered. Suddenly, it started
to rain. "And rainstorms," he added miserably.

Fabrico opened his new gadget. "This will keep
us dry. Come on, everybody squeeze together." After
a while, it began to pour. Not even Fabrico's gadget
could shelter us from the downpour. I shook the water
from my beak.

"Where did that remote control come from?" I asked.

"It fell from the sky!" explained Left.

"A fireball that went *kaaaaaboom*!" said Fabrico.

Something about the image of the fireball seemed familiar, but I brushed the feeling aside and concentrated on the problem facing us. *What were we going to do about the remote control – and Diggs?*

"I guess it doesn't matter where it came from. The important thing is to get it out of Diggs's hands!"

"Do you have a plan?" asked Right.

"Not really," I replied.

Suddenly, Fabrico began to hop from foot to foot, splashing rainwater everywhere.

"I have an idea!" he cried. "If I use this as a shield, I could get near enough to Diggs to seize the remote control!" The purple fellow couldn't wait to put his plan into action.

"Wait, Fabrico!" I called out.

But Fabrico was already halfway up the hill. Besides, even if he was willing to listen to my advice, he couldn't possibly hear it through the pounding rain. Helplessly, I shook my head and watched him go.

Left whispered something in Right's ear.

"Oh yes!" the right head exclaimed. "That's a great idea!"

"What idea?" I asked.

"Why don't we make the Grand Master of the Climate an offer he can't refuse!" the left head said.

The right head continued. "We'll bake him a special cake – a poisoned cake!"

Shocked, my beak fell open. 3R-V was equally stunned. Neither of us could find words to describe the heads' twisted plan.

A thunder clap shook us all, and a few seconds later, Fabrico fell at our feet.

"Not to worry, I'm fine," he said, coughing. He let out a puff of smoke. "My little shield and I are safe and sound!" Fabrico rose shakily to his feet. "You heads look like you're plotting something. Do you have a plan?"

"They do have a plan, but it's not a good one. They want to poison Diggs!" 3R-V said.

"Why, that's an excellent idea! What kind of poison do you suggest? Arsenic?"

3R-V and I couldn't believe what we were hearing. Our friends had lost their minds.

"Arsenic? Of course not, Fabrico!" said the right head. I was very relieved.

The left head explained. "We weren't thinking of giving Diggs anything dangerous, just a potion that will put him to sleep! I can make it from the red flower that blooms high on the mountain."

"Not the red flower," said Fabrico. "There's no way that I'm climbing back up that mountain to pick another flower! Don't look at me!"

"It's okay, Fabrico. Calm down. You don't need to go back," Right assured him.

"Right and I kept the red flower you brought back. We'll bake a cake and give it to Diggs as a peace offering. Once he falls asleep, all we have to do is take the remote control away from him," said Left.

Suddenly, the two-heads' idea didn't seem crazy after all.

"Are all of you ready to help?" the right head asked us.

Fabrico, 3R-V, and I nodded. We followed the two-heads to where the laboratory had once stood. It was in a million pieces. The two-heads searched the rubble for its recipe book.

"Here it is!" The left head was ready to cry. "This is awful. The page is ruined and the oven doesn't work either!"

"Hey, don't give up. Be creative!" said the right head.

Left scratched his head and thought hard. "Aha! I have a solution: we'll use 3R-V's engines to bake the cake."

"Great idea!" said 3R-V, happy to help.

"The cake has to be chocolate," insisted the right head. "Diggs won't be able to resist chocolate icing!" 3R-V agreed.

The two-heads lined up the ingredients.

"We have no time to lose. Let's get to work!" The two-heads gripped the red flower.

CHAPTER ELEVEN

Mission C. C. F. D.

Everything was in place for Mission C. C. F. D. (Chocolate Cake for Diggs). Fabrico went with the two-heads to deliver the cake and to act as a messenger. He would keep us posted about every step of the mission.

I was sheltered from the snow under a broad leaf, but the weather was growing worse.

"Look, 3R-V. The clouds are turning darker and darker. They better get that cake to Diggs soon."

"Remember the first planet, Cosmo? It was a wasteland. If the storms don't stop, the traveling planet will be a wasteland too."

"I sure hope this idea works. We have to stop Diggs, and soon. He's ruining this beautiful planet."

A gust of wind lifted the leaf from over my head. Fat snowflakes surrounded 3R-V and me.

"All this is the remote control's fault! It has no place on our traveling planet!" raged 3R-V.

"On the other hand, the remote may be our only way of bringing back the sun," I said.

The trees were bending in the wind, when Fabrico stuck his head through the leaves. "Diggs has taken the two-heads as prisoner!" he yelled.

"What do you mean! What happened?" 3R-V said.

"Tell us the whole story," I said to Fabrico. But he could barely breathe, let alone speak.

"Did it give the cake to Diggs?" I asked him. Fabrico nodded.

"And did Diggs eat it?" asked 3R-V. He nodded again.

"Did he discover the secret ingredient?" continued 3R-V.

Finally, Fabrico spoke: "Yes!"

"How could that happen?" I asked, perplexed.

"It was the lizard's fault," Fabrico explained.

I frowned. "How in the world did the lizard find out?"

"You know how Diggs dotes on her? He gave her a bite of the cake before he tasted it."

"Oh, no!" said 3R-V.

"Oh, yes. The lizard curled right up and fell asleep."

"What happened next?" I asked Fabrico.

He continued. "Diggs was very angry. He pointed the remote at the two-heads and turned it into one big ice statue!"

"Poor thing," said 3R-V.

"What are we going to do?" Fabrico turned to 3R-V and me.

"I could charge straight at him," said 3R-V, "if it weren't for his lightning bolts."

"That's it, 3R-V! I know what to do!"

"What are you talking about, Cosmo?"

There was no time to explain. All I could say was, "We need to get to Diggs's hill!"

CHAPTER TWELVE

The Shield

Black clouds pushed the gray clouds aside. Darkness was spreading, and the air became heavy. It was the calm before the storm!

On the way up Diggs's hill, the rain mixed with hail, snow, and lightning. 3R-V led the way to the top. We trekked along a path that was icy and dangerous.

Finally, we were close to the top. "I see Diggs," whispered 3R-V.

Fabrico, 3R-V, and I crawled to a rock, slicked over with ice, to take a look. Diggs had his back to us, the lizard was still asleep, and the two-heads, holding the remains of its cake, were frozen in a block of ice.

I turned to 3R-V.

"Are you ready?"

The robot-ship said a quiet "yes" and took off toward the sunny patch surrounding Diggs. Quickly, Diggs aimed the remote control at the two-heads, frozen in its ice cube.

"Take another step, 3R-V, and it's good-bye to your friends, Left and Right, forever!"

"You wouldn't dare, Diggs!" said 3R-V.

"It's Grand Master Diggs to you!" he corrected. *"Grrr!"*

3R-V wasn't about to give up. "Right and Left are your friends too."

"Friends? Bah! They tried to poison me! Look at my poor little lizard."

"Don't worry, she's only sleeping! She hasn't been hurt," 3R-V reassured him.

3R-V had Diggs's attention. It was time for Fabrico and me to get to work. We tiptoed over to the giant ice cube. I took a quick look back at 3R-V. The robot-ship met my glance, and he blinked twice. My plan was working!

I signalled to Fabrico. With a mighty heave, he pushed the ice block over the side of the hill. It slid down the hill with Fabrico and me on top of it. We hurtled at top speed down toward the valley!

"I'll try to slow us down with my super parachute!"
said Fabrico.

CHAPTER THIRTEEN

Save the Planet, Cosmo!

Our mad plunge down the hill came to a stop when we crashed into a boulder. The ice shattered, freeing the two-heads. It scrambled to its feet and we all hid behind the rock. We didn't need shelter from the rain or snow – we needed shelter from Diggs.

Back on the hilltop, the brave robot-ship prepared to charge Diggs.

"Stay back, 3R-V, or I'll unleash a lightning bolt on the two-heads."

"Oh no, you won't, Diggs!"

Diggs spun around, but the ice statue was gone! The Climate Master realized that he no longer had any power over 3R-V.

3R-V stepped toward Diggs. "Give me the remote control, please. Don't make me have to take it by force."

Frantically, Diggs aimed the remote at 3R-V and punched the lightning button.

3R-V nimbly stepped aside. The bolts came faster, but each time the little robot-ship was able to dart out of way. But the bolts came even faster until one caught 3R-V, full force. I watched in horror. "Oh no, 3R-V has been hit!"

3R-V lay upside down and perfectly still.

"You are not indestructible, after all. This is what happens to anyone who challenges my power!" Diggs crowed, standing over the fallen robot-ship.

Suddenly 3R-V snaked out a hand and yanked Diggs's ankle. Diggs fell to the ground with a *thump*. 3R-V scooped up the remote control. "I have it, Cosmo!"

Diggs got up and lunged at the robot-ship. But, 3R-V took off. Diggs reached for him, but missed and fell on his face. 3R-V jetted over and tossed the remote control to me as he landed.

"Good job, 3R-V!" I glanced back at the clouds. They had covered the sun. A gust of wind chilled us.

"Quick, how does this work?" I asked the two-heads.

While I was trying to work the remote control, Diggs appeared with his wide-awake and very angry lizard.

"*Grrr!* Give me back the remote, Cosmo!" he demanded.

"No, Diggs! The power makes you do crazy things!"

Diggs tried to grab me, but 3R-V blocked his way. Diggs saw that there was no use in fighting us. He crossed his arms and pouted.

"What are you waiting for, Cosmo? *Grrr!*" he grumbled. "If you're keeping the remote control, at least, clear away all these clouds!"

I pointed the remote at the clouds and pressed the sun symbol. Instead of sunshine, more and more black clouds appeared above us.

"I'm not so sure that's a good idea, Cosmo," said 3R-V. "Besides, it doesn't seem to be working."

"We can't let the storm take over this planet," I replied. "You saw the damage it caused the others."

"I know," said 3R-V. "But I still don't like the idea of controlling the climate."

"It's our only solution!" I pressed the sun button again, but still nothing happened. The black clouds thickened. "It's broken!"

CHAPTER FOURTEEN

Testing, One-Two-Three

"What's happened?!" the others cried.

"The remote control is not working!" I replied.

"Show it to me, Cosmo!" said the left head.

I handed it over, and Left pressed the sun button hard. The clouds went even darker.

"You're doing it wrong," said Right. He took the remote and pressed hard on the sun button, just as the left head had done.

"You're going to break it. Give it back to me!" While the heads squabbled, the clouds gathered, black and thick.

"Stop! This isn't the time to argue," I said, exasperated.

The two-heads silently handed the remote control to me, but Fabrico grabbed it out of my hand. "I can fix it!"

"Ridiculous!" growled Diggs. "I'm the only one who should be using it!"

"You are not to touch it anymore, Diggs!" declared 3R-V.

"Grrr!"

Above our heads, the black clouds swirled. Lightning streaked across the sky.

Fabrico peered intently at the remote. After a few moments, he opened his umbrella and started a rain shower.

"What are you doing?!" demanded Diggs.

"I'm demonstrating that this small object can prevent the rain from reaching me. Look, I am dry, but you are not! *Ha, ha, ha!*"

"You dope! It's an umbrella! Its whole purpose is to protect you from the rain." Diggs sneered.

The purple fellow peeked at Diggs from under the umbrella. "It's much more than that! It's a small multifunctional object."

Exasperated, I asked, "Fabrico, did you find out what's wrong with the remote control?"

"No, I can't figure it out. When I pressed the rain symbol, it worked." Fabrico shrugged.

The left head spoke up. "It's the sun button that doesn't work anymore. Every time we press on it, the weather gets worse."

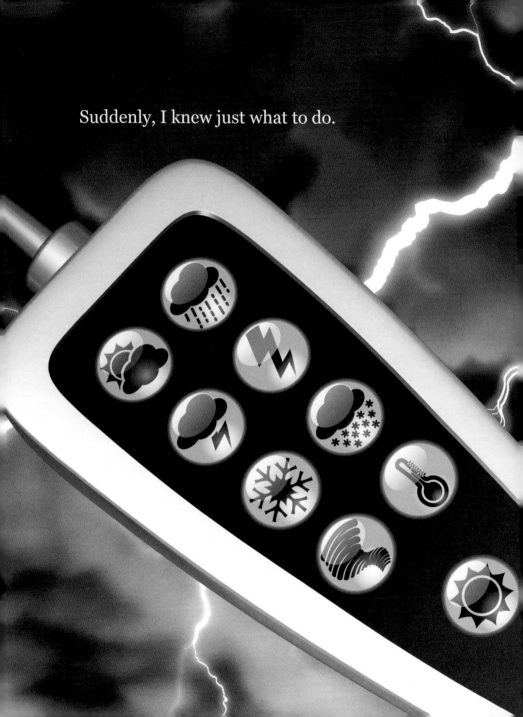

Suddenly, I knew just what to do.

CHAPTER FIFTEEN

Indestructible

I held up the remote. "The more we try to control the climate with it, the more unstable the Traveling planet's environment becomes."

Everyone thought about it.

"That makes sense!" said 3R-V.

"Yes, of course! The climate is not supposed to be controlled. Everything is a question of balance. When we use the remote, we destroy the balance," said the left head.

"That's why I was so uneasy about using it," added 3R-V.

We all looked from the remote control to the black clouds swirling above our heads. Thunder rumbled close by. A strong gust of wind lifted my feathers.

"We have to destroy the remote control before it devastates our planet for good! We can't play with the climate anymore," I said.

"If we don't allow anyone – or anything – to change it," replied Left, "the climate will probably go back to normal on its own."

I threw the remote control to the ground. 3R-V stomped on it with a metallic foot. Nothing happened. It wasn't even dented.

3R-V jumped on it with both feet. The robot-ship pounded and crushed and smushed the remote, but he could not destroy it. The wind howled as we tried to figure out what to do next.

"Uh . . . friends?" Fabrico tried to get our attention.

"*Shush!* We're concentrating, Fabrico!" said Right.

"Everyone, watch out!" he cried.

Fabrico's warning cry was too late. A blast of wind threw us all to the ground. Only 3R-V stood on his feet.

"What a gale!" shouted the left head.

"A gust that could ruffle even a stone statue!" the right head said poetically.

"Where did the wind come from?!" I yelled.

"I tried to warn you all!" shouted Fabrico. "It's coming from over there."

Lightning lit up the sky. That's when we all saw a tornado bearing down on us.

While we stared in horror, Diggs saw his chance. He pounced on the remote control.

"Ha, ha, ha!"

I jumped when I heard Diggs's laugh.

"Diggs, please, don't use the remote. It's the reason the climate is out of control on our traveling planet," I cried.

"You're making that up," replied Diggs.

"If you don't believe me, look for yourself! See, look at the black clouds and ... and that tornado!"

"This is nothing!" snorted Diggs. "One click and everything will be fine."

He pointed the remote at the sky and pressed the sun button.

"Nooooo!" we all cried together.

The tornado hit us.

Finally, Diggs understood. As we were all pulled by the tornado, he shoved the remote control into my hand.

Blasts of wind whipped our faces as we struggled to not get swept into the funnel. Diggs and I clung to each other. 3R-V held onto the two-heads and Fabrico. Suddenly, I had an idea. I let go of Diggs.

"Cosmo!" cried the others as I was pulled away. 3R-V stretched his hand toward me and grabbed my foot.

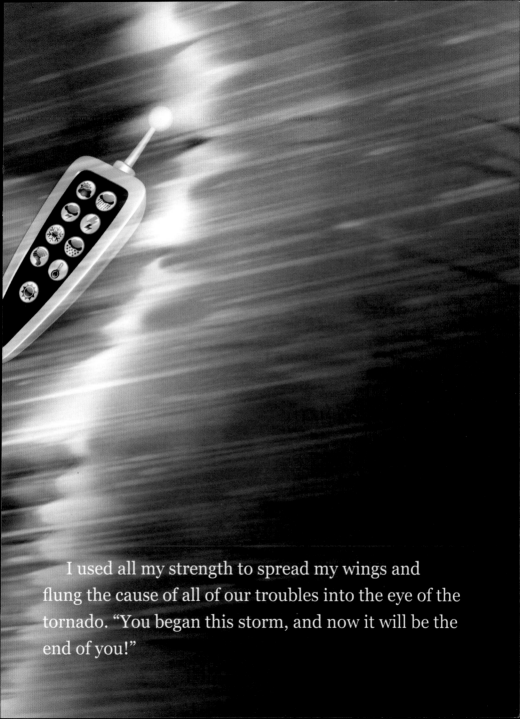

I used all my strength to spread my wings and flung the cause of all of our troubles into the eye of the tornado. "You began this storm, and now it will be the end of you!"

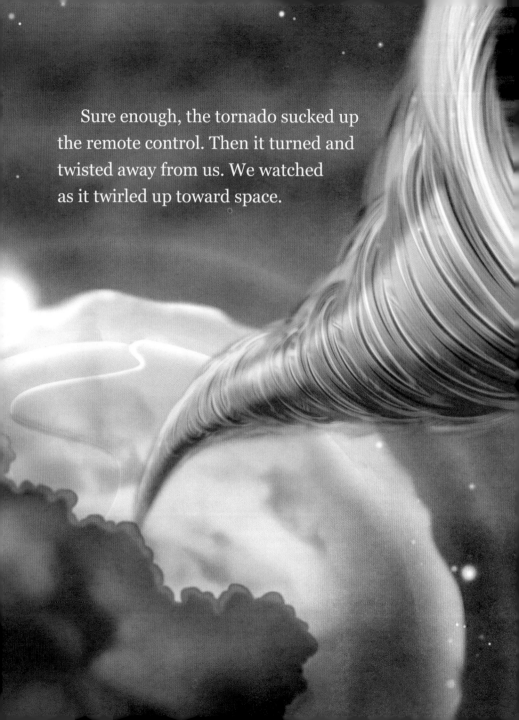

Sure enough, the tornado sucked up the remote control. Then it turned and twisted away from us. We watched as it twirled up toward space.

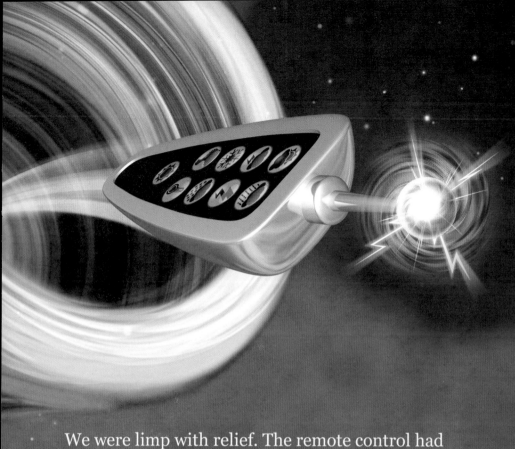

We were limp with relief. The remote control had disappeared, along with the tornado.

"Hooray!" we cheered when the wind died down.

"The traveling planet is saved!" I cried.

"Saved for good, or just for now?" asked Fabrico.

"We can only hope," said 3-RV. "But I have a feeling our adventures aren't over, yet."

THE QUEST OF THE LAST DODO BIRD
The last dodo bird on Earth, Cosmo, is running for his life when something amazing happens. 3R-V, a robot-spaceship from the future, hurtles down from space and rescues him. 3R-V's mission is to travel back in time and save endangered species from extinction. 3R-V and Cosmo, set off to explore the universe in search of other dodos.

THE TRAVELING PLANET
Cosmo the dodo bird and his friend 3R-V find and land on a traveling planet that has been blown out of its galaxy by a huge galactic tornado. Before they know it, they, along with a strange group of castaways, are in excitement. The new friends learn from each other and realize they have been given a second chance to protect their new environment.

THE CLIMATE MASTERS
When a strange object is discovered on the traveling planet, the friends find that they can change the climate with the push of a button! It doesn't take long before they have a planet-sized problem on their hands. The balance of nature has been destroyed, and Cosmo comes up with the solution to stop the damage before it's too late . . . or does he?!

THE CHAIN REACTION
The adventure continues when it becomes apparent that the climate is now completely out of control. One catastrophe leads to another, putting the friends' lives in danger. With the traveling planet in ruins, should they abandon their once-beautiful home or put selfish-ness aside and work to restore it?

For more cosmic fun, go to
www.cosmothedodobird.com